10|11

Kenji and the Magic Geese

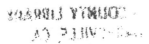

Kenji and the Magic Geese

by Ryerson Johnson

illustrated by Jean and Mou-sien Tseng

SIMON & SCHUSTER BOOKS FOR YOUNG READERS

Published by Simon & Schuster
New York • London • Toronto • Sydney • Tokyo • Singapore

The first thing Kenji saw every morning was the picture of the flying geese. The birds looked almost alive. He liked to count them: "One…two…three…four…*five*."

Every year when the wild geese flew over his house in Japan, Kenji would laugh and tease his picture geese. "Just flying halfway up on the wall of my room—sometime wouldn't you like to fly high with the wild geese?"

One year it rained so much that the water crawled out of the river and crept inside the houses. Poor Kenji! Water wet his books and made the pages stick together. It even floated away some of his toys. Fortunately, the water did not rise high enough to harm the picture of the five geese.

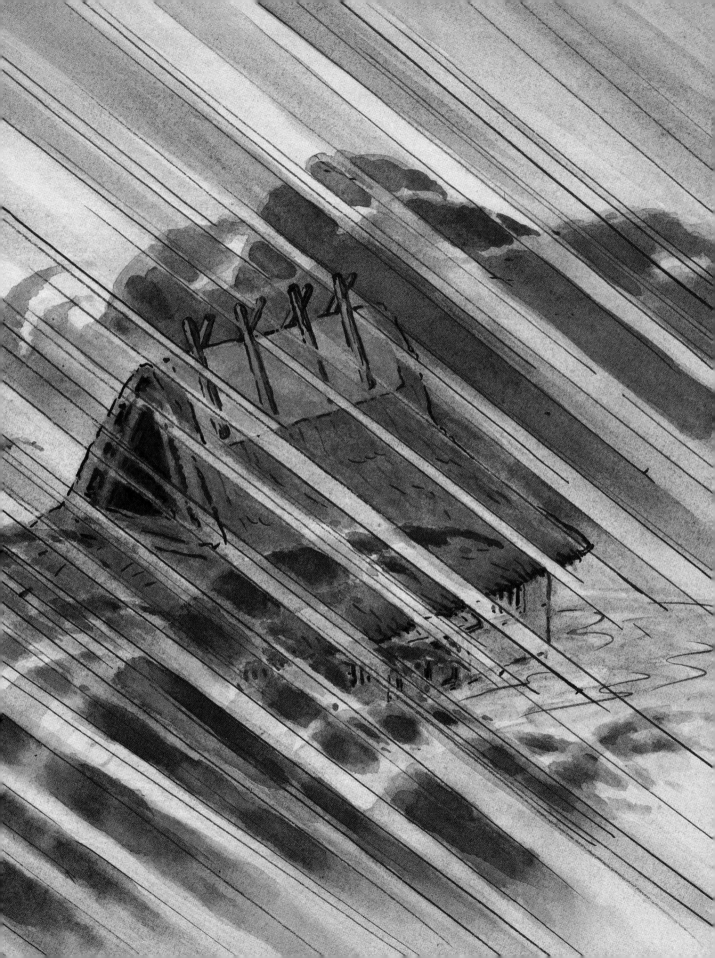

When the water went back to the river, Kenji went out to his muddy yard to play in the bamboo. He looked up when a fussy old man knocked with his cane at their door. The man had thick, round glasses on a sharp nose. Kenji thought he looked like an owl—a hungry one!

Kenji hid in the bamboo until the owl-man went away.

"Father," he asked, "who was that man?"

"An art collector," his father said. "Someone who buys pictures. The flood has washed away our rice houses, Kenji-*san*. We must sell the picture to buy food."

Kenji wanted to cry. He liked this picture more than anything. He knew his parents liked it, too. It had been painted by a famous artist almost three hundred years ago.

On the day the art collector was coming to take away the picture, Kenji heard the wild geese calling *honk-honk...honk-honk* as they flew over the town on their long way south.

"Before you have to go and live in that old collector's house," he said to the geese in the picture, "I'll give you something to remember—a ride high in the sky with the wild geese."

Carefully, carefully, he pasted the picture on his biggest kite.

Up and up the kite went, high above trees and houses. *Honk-honk-honk*, the wild geese called. The kite pulled hard in the wind, as though the geese in the picture were trying to fly out and join those wild ones.

When Kenji pulled down his kite, he saw something
extraordinary. *Five* geese had gone up on the kite. Only *four*
had come down. The big goose, the one that he called Yuki,
was missing!

Yuki has gone with the wild geese, Kenji decided.

The art collector did not believe it. *"Arr-rr-rr!"* he growled. "A four-goose picture. Everyone knows that there should be *five* geese. Someone has scraped off the biggest goose. The picture is ruined!"

He stamped his cane and went away.

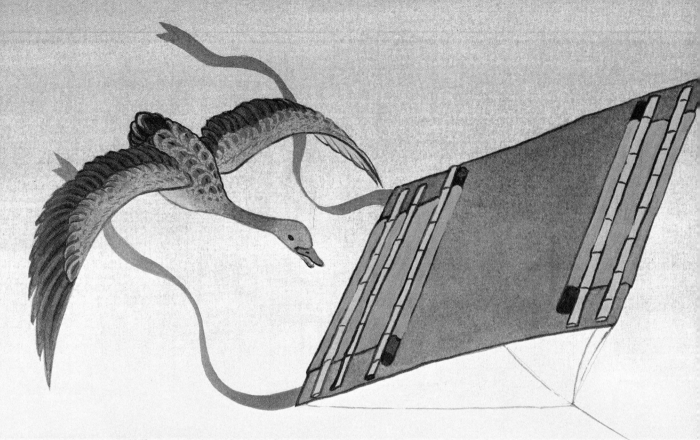

That night there was nothing to eat but a little rice. No *misu* soup, no buckwheat noodles, no tofu or moon-in-the-window cakes.

The long winter passed. Even the wind sounded hungry as it whimpered around the house like a starved puppy. And the wild geese sounded sad as they called *honk-honk* from high in the sky on their way north again.

When he heard the geese, Kenji sat up straight. Then he hurried to take the picture from the wall and paste it on his kite.

Everything happened just the way he hoped. He felt a tug on his kite string; and when he pulled down the kite, there were five geese in the picture! He counted to make sure: "One...two...three...four...*five!*"

He ran to tell his parents that Yuki had come back.

Kenji's bewildered father stored the picture away safely in a closet. Then he wrote to the art collector.

This time when the art collector saw the picture, his arms swung around like the tails of a kite on a windy day. "Arr-rr-rr!" he growled. "Last time I found the great artist's picture ruined because a goose was gone. This time it is ruined by childish scribbling!"

He stamped his cane and went away angrily.

Poor Kenji's father stood rubbing his head where the hair used to be. There *were* strange marks on the picture—marks that would not rub off.

Even Kenji did not know what to say about this.

Late that night he woke up. "I hear funny sounds," he called to his parents. "Chip-chipping sounds. They seem to come from the closet."

"Stand back everybody," Kenji's father said. He opened the door.

"Look at the picture!" Kenji shouted.

The marks that wouldn't rub off—two lopsided circles—were gone. In their place were two baby goslings. They didn't move. They were just there, as the artist might have painted them.

"I know!" Kenji said. "Those marks on the picture were Yuki's eggs!"

Kenji's father wrote another letter to the art collector.

This time the man's owlish eyes opened wide with surprise and pleasure. His lips snapped together like a hungry boy's chopsticks as he said, "A masterpiece! In perfect condition. No geese missing, no childish scribbling. Five geese flying and two little ones swimming. Everyone knows about the *five*-goose picture. But no one has heard of this *seven*-goose one. You have made a great discovery!"

The man took out his money, but Kenji's father said, "Thanking you, honorable sir, but my wife and I and our little boy have decided not to sell the picture. You would put it away in your big house where no one would see it. Such a fine picture should be enjoyed by all."

"*Arr-rr-rr-rr-RR!*" the art collector roared. He stamped his cane and turned to leave.

"Wait," Kenji's father said. "You have the honor to be the first to pay—one sen. This is the only picture with seven geese in it. One sen is a price so small that all can pay. I think people will come from everywhere in Japan to see the picture. They may even come from China and America."

The news spread. People *did* come to see the picture. But no one could agree about the size of the two goslings.

Kenji explained. "They are growing, that's all."

"How can geese grow in a picture?" he was asked often.

Kenji just shrugged. "I think they grow only when no one is looking."

Time went by. And then one moonlit autumn night, the wild geese flew over the house again on their long trip south. Kenji went to sleep hearing their exciting, faraway, lonely call.

He dreamed that one of the wild geese flew down and made soft honking sounds just outside the open window, and that there was a quick stirring in the dark room and something brushed his cheek.

In the morning his mother asked, "How did you get that little scratch on your cheek, Kenji-*san?*"

Kenji did not even feel the scratch, but he became excited when he counted the geese in the picture. "One…two…three …four…*five*—and that's all! So it wasn't a dream."

Kenji was not sad about the two young geese flying away. "They will come back in the spring," he told everybody, "because they will want to stay part of the time with their father and the wild geese, and part of the time with their mother, Yuki, and me—halfway up on my wall."

To Robie, David, and Brennan — R J

In memory of my mother, Lin Lou,
a woman of great courage — MST

SIMON & SCHUSTER BOOKS FOR YOUNG READERS, Simon & Schuster Building, Rockefeller Center
1230 Avenue of the Americas, New York, New York 10020. Text copyright © 1992 by Ryerson Johnson, Illustrations
© 1992 by Jean Tseng and Mou-sien Tseng. All rights reserved including the right of reproduction in whole or in part in
any form. SIMON & SCHUSTER BOOKS FOR YOUNG READERS is a trademark of Simon & Schuster. Designed by
Lucille Chomowicz. The text of this book is set in 16 point Weiss. The illustrations were done in watercolor. Manufactured
in the United States of America.

10 9 8 7 6 5 4 3 2

Library of Congress Cataloging-in-Publication Data. Johnson, Ryerson, 1901– Kenji and the magic geese / by
Ryerson Johnson ; illustrated by Jean and Mou-sien Tseng. Summary: One of the geese in the beloved picture on Kenji's
wall flies off to join the wild geese in the sky and then returns to the picture, with interesting results. [1. Geese—
Fiction. 2. Art—Fiction. 3. Japan—Fiction.] I. Tseng, Jean, ill. II. Tseng, Mou-sien, ill. III. Title. PZ7.J6366Ke
1992 [E]—dc20 91-36448 CIP

ISBN: 0-671-75974-4